Patrick
July 98

ABOUT THE AUTHOR

Christopher Pike was born in New York, but grew up in Los Angeles, where he still lives. Prior to becoming a writer he worked in a factory, painted houses and programmed computers. His hobbies include astronomy, meditating, running and making sure his books are prominently displayed in his local bookshop. As well as being a best-selling children's writer, he is also the author of three adult novels.

Spooksville

1 The Secret Path
2 The Howling Ghost
3 The Haunted Cave
4 Aliens in the Sky
5 The Cold People
6 The Witch's Revenge
7 The Dark Corner
8 The Little People
9 The Wishing Stone
10 The Wicked Cat
11 The Deadly Past
12 The Hidden Beast
13 Alien Invasion
14 The Evil House
15 Invasion of the No Ones
16 Time Terror
17 The Thing in the Closet
18 Attack of the Giant Crabs
19 Night of the Vampire
20 The Dangerous Quest
21 Return of the Dead
22 The Creepy Creature

Spooksville

ATTACK OF THE

GIANT CRABS

Christopher Pike

*Hodder
Children's
Books*

a division of Hodder Headline plc

First published in Great Britain in 1997
by Hodder Children's Books
a division of Hodder Headline plc
338 Euston Road
London NW1 3BH

This edition published in 1998

A Catalogue record for this book is available from the British Library

ISBN 0 340 72446 3

Typeset by Avon Dataset Ltd, Bidford-on-Avon, Warks

Printed and bound in Great Britain by
Mackays of Chatham, Chatham, Kent

One

The gang was down at the beach. They were all there: Adam Freeman; Sally Wilcox; Cindy Makey; Watch; Bryce Poole; George Sanders; Tira Jones. Of course George and Tira were relatively new to the group, but the others were beginning to spend more time with them. They had done ever since George and Tira had helped them with The Thing In the Closet – those wicked Shadow creatures from Zeta's realm.

Tira was a true delight to be around, with her great beauty and sweet personality. Not to mention her occasional intuitive insights. George was also good company, considering he was a newcomer to

Spooksville. He was literally afraid of *everything*. Sally had a lot of fun with him. Sally had been looking for a new target ever since Cindy had got wise to her.

'George, you have to be careful down here,' Sally said as they walked along the beach. The day was sunny but cold. A stiff breeze blew from the north, causing the tips of the waves to foam with icy froth. It was a Friday evening; the sun would set in a couple of hours. Sally walked beside George as she spoke; she was a full head taller than him. The others trailed behind. Sally pointed to the choppy water. 'These waters are full of great white sharks. A lot of kids have lost limbs swimming here.'

George looked suitably frightened but tried to put on a brave front.

'I don't have to worry about sharks,' he said. 'I never go into the water. I can't swim.'

Sally smiled. 'Do you have PE at school?'

'Of course. We all do.'

'Well in PE they make you learn to swim. In fact, they make you swim down here. Last year in my class alone we lost three students and four legs and two arms.'

George shook his head. 'I don't believe that.'

'It's true,' Sally said. 'You're going to learn to swim whether you want to or not. Either that or you drown. But don't worry – I know a way to avoid the sharks.'

Now George was interested.

'How?' he asked.

'Just smear yourself with cat fur before you get in the water. All fish – big and small – are afraid of cats. It's instinctive. I can sell you some fur if you don't have any. I run a cat-shaving business on the side, you know.'

George frowned. 'How much is it?'

'You have to buy it by the kilogram. If you're hoping to drive off a great white, you should have at least two kilograms on you.' Sally paused. 'That will be fifty bucks.'

George was worried. 'I don't have that much.'

'It doesn't matter. You're a friend. I can work out a payment plan.'

'When do the swimming lessons start at school?'

'The teachers never tell you. One day they just drive you down here and throw you in the water.' Sally pointed to the nearby pier. 'Sometimes they dump you off the pier.'

'That sounds cruel,' George said.

'It works. You either sink or swim. Hey, I think I can give you the cat fur for forty bucks. Do you have that much?'

George hesitated. 'Maybe. But why is it so much?'

'Because forty bucks just happens to be exactly how much Sally needs to buy that new dress she saw in the store window an hour ago,' Cindy said from behind them, with a laugh. George turned to look at her. Cindy had blonde hair and blue eyes and was always trying to protect others from Sally.

'Is Sally pulling my leg again?' he asked.

'Not as hard as those sharks will,' Sally said.

Adam smiled. 'Of course she is, George. Think – how is cat fur going to protect you from a great white shark? The idea is ridiculous. You are just too gullible.' Adam had only moved to Spooksville the previous summer but he was the unquestioned leader of the group. He was brave and resourceful.

George was annoyed with Sally. 'Would you really have taken my money?' he asked.

'Sure, if you were stupid enough to give it to me,' Sally said.

'But I am new here,' George protested. 'I don't know what is real and what isn't. I wouldn't believe any of this stuff you tell me if I hadn't already been attacked by a ghost and an alien.'

'Look on the bright side,' Watch said. 'You are growing up fast.' Watch was the smartest one in the group, and in some ways the most mysterious. He seemed to live by himself and always wore four watches at the same time, each one set to a different U.S. time zone.

'I was only two months old when a werewolf tried to eat me,' Bryce Poole said. Bryce was also resourceful, and handsome, but he had a tendency to show off. Still, the others in the gang trusted him – he had helped save their lives a number of times.

'What did you do?' Cindy asked.

'Squirted him with my bottle,' Bryce said.

'I'm surprised that drove the werewolf off,' Sally said.

5

'It was only a baby werewolf,' Bryce admitted. 'And I think the milk in the bottle was sour.'

'I was only a month old when I was attacked by a vampire,' Sally said.

'How did you scare it off?' Cindy asked. 'Did you show it your cute baby face?'

Sally scowled. 'No, this is a true story. I had to grab a mirror and reflect sunlight in its pale face.' She added, 'I also had to scream really loudly. Vampires can't stand screaming babies. It makes their blood boil.'

'I'm glad I wasn't born here,' George said miserably.

'But you'll probably die here,' Sally said brightly. 'Not many kids here live to be adults. If a shark doesn't get you, something else will.'

'I think we will all live to old age,' Tira said quietly. Tira was old herself. Although she appeared to be only twelve, she was actually two centuries old. But because she had spent most of that time possessed by an alien spirit – about which she could remember nothing nowadays – she had not aged beyond twelve years.

'I hope we will,' Adam said, staring at the ocean water. He lifted his arm and pointed to a spot straight out in front of them, a hundred metres offshore. 'Am I imagining it, or is something huge churning the water right there?'

Adam was imagining nothing. There was definitely something large beneath the water. Something moving in such a way that the waves were being distorted on the surface. Yet, because of the salt water and the turbulence, they could not see it clearly. The gang crept closer to the water's edge and peered at it. All of them, that is, except George.

'That is strange,' Sally said. 'Could it be a whale?'

Watch peered through his thick glasses. He couldn't see a thing without them. He frowned as he studied the sea water.

'I don't think it is a whale,' he said. 'Notice how the water seems to be spiralling. I don't think a whale, no matter how big, would make that happen.' He paused. 'Maybe it's a submarine.'

'A submarine would never come in this close,' Bryce noted.

'That is true,' Watch said. 'Unless their

7

navigational instruments were broken.'

'As far as I can tell,' Adam said, 'it seems to be round. I've never seen a round submarine before.'

'It could be a flying saucer,' Sally suggested.

'Gimme a break,' Cindy said.

'Why are you so sceptical?' Sally demanded. 'You've been in a flying saucer.'

'I know that,' Cindy agreed. 'But don't they usually stick to the air and deep space?'

'Look,' Adam said. 'I think it's beginning to come up.'

A coloured dome began to push above the surface.

It had an odd texture. It did not look metal.

The gang moved slowly backwards. The dome emerged further.

They saw huge eyes. Giant claws.

'It's a crab!' Cindy screamed.

'It's a monster!' Sally yelled.

It was both. The crab had to be ten metres across. Even though it must have been in pretty deep water, it seemed to be standing. Its huge claws clicked in the air as its sickening eyes panned the beach. Its eyes were the worst part. Moist and hungry, there was something strange in their depth that made Adam think they were directed by an evil intelligence. A cold wave swept over him as they locked on him.

The crab made a thin screeching sound and rushed towards them.

The gang turned and fled.

Except for George, they realised a moment later.

He stood frozen in horror, whimpering to himself.

'Wait!' Adam cried, stopping and turning. 'It's going to get George!'

'It's going to get all of us!' Sally yelled back, tugging at Adam's shirt. 'Let's get out of here.'

Adam shook her off. 'I have to save him,' he said. 'You guys get off the beach.'

Before they could protest further, Adam ran off in the direction of George. When he reached him the giant crab was only ten metres away. Tears streamed down George's face as he stared at the crab, his eyes bulging. Adam had to slap him on the back to shake him from his shock.

'George!' Adam yelled. 'You have to run!'

'I don't want to die,' George moaned.

The giant crab was almost out of the water. Adam could hardly bear to look at it. He had never heard a sound more horrifying than the clicking of its claws.

Adam slapped George again.

'Stop sobbing and get your butt in gear!' Adam screamed. 'Or we're both going to die!'

George looked at him with a strange expression on his face.

'You're risking your life to save me,' he whispered.

'Not any more!' Adam shouted as he turned and ran towards the others, who were waiting for him where the sand met the road. To Adam's immense relief, he heard George running after him.

'Wait!' George yelled.

'Keep running, Adam!' Sally shouted. 'It's getting closer!'

'You run!' Adam shouted and waved his arm as he raced towards his friends. To his surprise George drew even with him. The little guy really could move when he wanted to. Behind them the sound of the clicking claws grew even louder. Yet their bikes were not far away. If they could just reach them, Adam felt, they would be safe. Indeed, Watch and the others had already reached the bikes and were standing them up so that he and George could jump on them the moment they caught up.

'Faster!' Cindy screamed as Adam and George reached the sidewalk and turned in the direction of the bikes. Adam literally jumped on his bike at a full run. George seemed to do likewise. The pedalled so hard that in seconds they were up to full speed. Behind them, thankfully, they heard the clicking of the giant crab's claws grow fainter. Adam risked a glance over his shoulder.

The giant crab had given up and was heading back towards the water.

In a few seconds it was back in the water, sinking beneath the surface.

The rest of the beach was empty.

It seemed no one else had seen the crab except them.

They slowed their bikes, paused to catch their breath.

'We are going to have to warn everyone about that crab,' Adam said, panting. 'It could come back.'

'I don't think anyone will believe us,' Sally warned.

She was right, at least for a little while.

Two

George wanted to go to the police and tell them about the giant crab. The others had to explain – for the tenth time – that the police in Spooksville seldom left the police station for fear of being killed.

'You have to rely on yourself in this town,' Sally said to George as they regrouped not far from the pier.

'There are two shops on the pier,' Adam said. 'It's possible some of the people who work there saw the crab. We should talk to them, convince them they'd better get off the pier for now.'

'That is a good idea,' Watch said. 'But we should

figure out what we're going to say if they haven't seen the crab.'

'We should just tell them the truth about what we saw,' Cindy said.

'But what did we see?' Watch said. 'It looked like a giant crab but that doesn't really say anything. What I mean is, I have never seen anything like it before.'

'You're asking where it came from,' Bryce said. 'Why it was so big.'

'Exactly,' Watch said. 'There must be a reason behind its giant size.'

'This is a weird town,' Sally said. 'There isn't a reason for half the things I've seen. Let's just warn people around here and then stay away from the beach for a while – like for the next year.'

Watch nodded, although he still seemed to be thinking deeply.

'I am for warning people as quickly as possible,' he said.

They rode their bikes on to the pier. One of the shops sold gifts, the other fish and chips. The latter had the best french fries in all of Spooksville, and they knew the owner pretty well. His name was Mr Seafish – or that was what everyone called him. About seventy, he looked and smelled like he had been born on a boat. His skin was so wrinkled from the sun that it was hard to see his nose and mouth. Still, he was a lot of fun, and often gave away free food if they were short on cash. He flashed a warm smile as they came pounding through his door.

'It's the gang,' he said with pleasure. 'I saw you guys down at the beach and was hoping you would stop by. Double chips today for everyone?'

'No,' Adam said seriously. 'You have to close your shop immediately and get off the pier.'

Mr Seafish blinked. He had practically no eyebrows, just intense blue eyes. It was said that he could draw fish to his net just by staring at the water. For sure, when he did go fishing in a small motor boat he kept anchored off the pier, he always came back with a big catch.

'Why do I have to get off the pier?' he asked.

'Did you see the giant crab that came up on to the beach?' Watch asked.

Mr Seafish scratched his bold head. 'What are

15

you talking about? I didn't see anything.'

'It was only on the beach for a few minutes,' Adam said. 'But it was huge, as big as a truck.'

'A truck with a trailer,' George added.

Mr Seafish smiled. 'Now that would be a sight. If there was such a thing.'

'We all saw it,' Sally said. 'You have to get out of here. We're not making this up. It might come back any second.'

Mr Seafish lost his smile. 'You kids are serious.'

Watch nodded. 'We have never been more serious. Do you know if Miss Crank is next door in the gift shop? We need to warn her as well.'

Mr Seafish shook his head and stepped over to the window at the rear of his small shop that overlooked the water and the beach.

'She went home an hour ago,' he said. 'When the weather is cold like this she doesn't get many customers.' He paused. 'I know you guys wouldn't lie to me, but I don't see anything.'

'It went back into the water,' Adam explained. 'But we can't exaggerate how big it was or how dangerous. It chased us all the way back to our bikes.'

16

'It almost ate George and Adam,' Tira added.

Despite what Mr Seafish said about trusting them, he seemed to have doubts. He glanced back at them.

'But I sometimes get a bunch of customers right now at dinner time,' he said. 'If I close up they'll be disappointed.'

'Better that they go a little hungry than you be someone else's dinner,' Bryce said darkly. 'Or some*thing's*.'

Mr Seafish seemed unconvinced.

'There doesn't seem to be any danger right now,' he said. 'Why don't I keep the shop open until seven instead of the usual nine? Most of my customers would have come by then.'

'We're risking our lives just by standing here and talking to you,' Sally complained. 'How can you talk about staying open another two hours?'

Sally's tone may have been too strong. Mr Seafish drew back.

'I'm not asking you to stay here,' he said. 'You're free to go.'

'Please,' Adam said with feeling. 'We can't just

leave you here. If the crab comes back this will probably be the first place it attacks.'

Mr Seafish smiled and patted a broomstick in the corner.

'Don't worry,' he said. 'If it does show up, I'll be able to beat it off.'

'You wouldn't be able to beat it off if you had a tent pole,' Sally said.

But the words were wasted on Mr Seafish. He had made up his mind, the shop would stay open. Feeling discouraged, the gang trudged out of his shop and slowly rode their bikes back to where the road met the pier. The sky was dark grey, still cloudy. As far as they could tell the sun had already set. A cold wind continued to blow from the north.

'I told you so,' Sally said, as she often did. They paused on their bikes as they reached the entrance to the pier.

'What are we going to do now?' Cindy asked.

'We have to get somebody to listen to us,' Adam said. 'But I hate to leave this area unprotected. We might have to split up.'

'We need weapons against these things,' Watch

said. 'Even if we all stay here, we won't be able to protect anyone.'

'Maybe we can get some guns from Mr Patton at his Army Surplus store,' Bryce said.

Sally nodded. 'A flame thrower would be good.'

'I still think we should talk to the police,' George said. 'If enough of us say we saw it, they will have to believe us.'

'We've already told you,' Sally said impatiently. 'Even if they do believe us, they won't do anything about it.'

George lowered his head. 'My mother always said I was supposed to trust the police.'

'Your mother has never seen a giant crab before,' Sally said.

'We have to stop arguing,' Tira said. 'It is clear we have to split up. Why don't Cindy and I stay here with Adam and wait for the return of the giant crab? You guys can go and get weapons and try to warn other people.'

'That sounds like an intelligent plan,' Adam said. 'George, if you must, you can even try the police.'

'George will probably ride straight home and

lock his front door,' Sally muttered.

'I had thought of that,' George admitted. 'But I will go to the police if no one else will.'

It was decided then. Sally, Watch and Bryce headed off in the direction of Mr Patton's Army Surplus store. George rode by himself towards the police station. Tira, Cindy and Adam set aside their bikes and waited at the entrance to the pier.

They had not been waiting long when the horror returned.

This time there were five giant crabs.

Three

The monsters came all at once, almost without warning. Adam first noticed the sea beginning to churn and then saw the giant crabs poking their ugly heads out of the water. In seconds they had moved to the beach. Once again, their ugly moist eyes scanned the area, looking for victims. Tira and Cindy reached for their bikes. Two of the crabs began to move in their direction, clicking their huge claws in the air.

'They can see us,' Cindy gasped.

'You two get out of here!' Adam ordered as he reached for his bike. 'Find the others, tell them what has happened.'

Tira grabbed his arm. 'Where are you going?' she asked.

He shook her off. 'I have to warn Mr Seafish. He is a sitting duck out on the pier.'

Cindy blocked Adam's way and stared at him with anxious eyes.

'If you try to save him you will be a sitting duck,' she said. 'You will get cut off. You'll have nowhere to run to.'

Adam tried to get past her. 'Let me go, there's no time. I can't just leave him to be killed.'

'If you're going, we're going with you,' Cindy said.

'No,' Adam said strongly.

'Yes,' Tira said firmly. 'Adam, you're right to want to save the man. But let's go now, before the crabs reach here.'

Adam shook his head. 'It makes no sense to risk all three of us. You guys go and get the others. They need warning.'

Cindy and Tira ignored him. They began to ride their bikes on to the pier, in the direction of the fish and chip shop. Adam had to pedal hard to catch them. They had wasted valuable seconds arguing. The two giant crabs that had spotted them were already half-way to the pier. They were exactly the same size and shape and colour. Both let out a thin screech at the same time.

When Adam and his friends reached Mr Seafish, he was calmly preparing fish to be fried. He had not even looked out of his window in the last few minutes, despite their warnings. But as they dashed into his shop, and he saw their horrified faces, his head immediately jerked to the window. His tan face turned white and the plate of fish in his hands fell to the floor and cracked.

'Oh no,' he gasped. 'It's true.'

'Hurry!' Adam yelled. 'We have to get off the pier before we are cut off.'

Mr Seafish didn't need any more prodding. He dashed around his counter and out on to the pier. He raced towards the entrance like a man of twenty running for the Olympic gold medal. They had to pedal hard to catch up. Yet, because they were on bikes, they had the advantage. A few seconds later they passed him at high speed. By then the two crabs were almost at the pier entrance. It looked like they might make it, but Mr Seafish still had a long way to run.

'Faster!' Adam shouted over his shoulder.

'Can't,' Mr Seafish gasped as he suddenly began to lose strength and slow down. He was, after all, seventy years old. Even the threat of the approaching crabs could not give strength to his legs and heart. Adam could see that if the three of them didn't slow down, they would definitely make it. Just the opposite, Mr Seafish was definitely not going to make it.

Unknown to the girls, Adam began to slow.

He turned his bike back towards the struggling Mr Seafish.

Tira and Cindy raced off the pier, with the crabs only fifteen metres from the entrance. The crabs moved fast but they could not catch two healthy girls on bikes. For the moment the girls were safe – the crabs didn't even try to go after them. The monsters now had eyes only for Adam and Mr Seafish. Over his shoulder, Adam saw the creatures step on to the pier and begin to move in their direction. The crabs slowed as they approached. Perhaps they knew that they had their poor human prey cornered, that there was no escape.

Adam also slowed as he reached Mr Seafish, who now stood panting, trying to recover from his unsuccessful dash. Mr Seafish continued to look pale but a weary expression of acceptance had also stolen over his face.

'It looks like they've got us,' he said to Adam. 'I wish I had listened to you guys to begin with. But I've never seen monsters like those before.'

The crabs continued to approach, clicking their claws.

Adam tried not to think about what it would be like to be eaten by them.

'We have to fight them off,' Adam said. 'We can't give up.'

Mr Seafish sighed. 'I don't see how we can stop them.'

Adam had an idea. 'I remember how you told us you kept a kerosene generator in the back of your shop because the salty air was always shorting out the normal power lines. Do you still have it?'

'Yes. It is running now. What do you want to do with it?'

'Let's drain the kerosene off in front of your shop and set it on fire just as the crabs attack. It might scare them off.'

Unlooked-for hope crossed Mr Seafish's face.

'It might work,' he said as he turned back towards his shop. 'But I'll need your help to lift the generator's fuel tank.'

They hurried back to the shop. Adam threw his bike down outside. Crouched over the generator and the fuel tank, they anxiously searched for the bolts that held it down. Yet outside they could see that the crabs were coming too quickly. They would never get the tank free in time. Adam stood back up.

'Let's just puncture the tank,' he said to Mr Seafish. 'We'll let the fuel flood the shop. When the crabs come in, we'll set it on fire.'

'But we'll burn to death.'

'No,' Adam said as he shoved open the rear window. 'We'll jump out the back just as we light the kerosene. If we hold on to the pier bars, we should be able to make it to safety.'

'But my shop will be destroyed. It's all I have.'

Adam glanced in the direction of the crabs. They were only fifty metres away and approaching swiftly.

'I think these monsters are going to destroy your shop anyway,' Adam said grimly. 'Quick, what can we use to puncture the fuel tank?'

Mr Seafish had a small tool kit under the front counter, which held a hammer and screwdriver. Placing the screwdriver in the centre of the tank, he pounded it hard. The steel went through the soft aluminium. The kerosene gushed on to the floor. In moments the shop was choked with fuel. The crabs were now thirty metres away.

'Do you have a lighter?' Adam asked as he coughed from the smell.

'I have wooden matches,' Mr Seafish said as he rifled through a crowded drawer. 'I just wish I could find them.'

Adam moved to the front door of the shop and slammed it shut. He knew it would not keep the crabs out. The fuel began to creep around his sneakers. Adam turned the lock on the door and stepped away from it. Outside the crabs reached the shop and began to poke at the door with their claws. Their hideous eyes peered through the shop windows and they clicked their claws with great excitement.

'Have you found those matches yet?' Adam asked desperately.

'Not yet.'

A claw smashed through the window on the right, showering Adam with broken glass. He had to raise his arm and shield his eyes to stop himself from going blind. The claw squeezed its way through the window. Adam felt something large and gross brush against his shirt. He jumped back behind the counter and reached for the broomstick. The claw swung over his head and he ducked. When he came up he smacked the claw with the stick and heard the crab screech again. For a moment it pulled its claw back out of the window.

'They will be through that door in a minute,' Adam said. 'We need those matches.'

Mr Seafish yanked open another jammed drawer.

'Still looking,' he said. 'Can you hold them off?'

'No! Look faster!'

One crab fastened its pinchers on to the door handle and began to pull. The wood groaned and splintered. The other crab stuck its claw back in the window, the left one this time. More glass flew through the shop. Adam picked up a steel pan and smashed the tip of the claw as it reached for his head. The crab did not withdraw. It snapped at his belly and Adam jumped back. Yet there was only so far back he could go. They were now both pinned to the rear of Mr Seafish's shop. Adam swung again with his pan, almost hitting Mr Seafish on the head.

'Mr Seafish!' Adam yelled.

The old man jerked upright, a box of matches in his hand.

'Got them!' he exclaimed. 'Should I light the fuel?'

'I'll light it,' Adam said, grabbing the matches. 'Climb out the back window – hang on to the railing. When the fire begins to burn, move up the railing towards the entrance of the pier.'

Mr Seafish was only too happy to climb out of the window. For a moment Adam was alone with the two crabs just outside the door. The door was actually not doing too well. Even as Adam moved towards the window, the bottom of it caved in and another claw snaked into the shop.

This one managed to grab Adam.

It fastened on his right leg and began to squeeze.

Adam felt faint. The pain was intense.

The entire door caved in and the crab opened its mouth wide. Adam felt himself falling. Felt himself being pulled into that mouth. Desperately he reached for anything within arm's reach. His hands landed on the fire extinguisher, which was fortunate. Turning the nozzle towards the approaching monster, he twisted the knob on top. A thin stream of white liquid, mixed with chemicals, shot into the crab's eyes. The monster released him and stepped back out of the shop, letting out an ear-piercing screech.

For a moment, Adam was free.

Then the other crab tried to squeeze into the shop.

Adam was through wrestling with the creatures. Ducking another swinging claw, he leapt towards the back window. Mr Seafish was already outside, hanging on to the railing that ran the length of the pier. Below them the darkening sea water churned. How many more monsters were down there, Adam wondered?

'Better get out here, son,' Mr Seafish advised.

'I'm coming,' Adam said as he pulled himself through the open window. As he did so a claw snapped at his bottom. Adam almost fell forwards – almost fell the fifteen metres into the water – he moved so fast. But a moment later he was outside in the cold wind with Mr Seafish, hanging on to the railing and trying to keep his feet on the narrow edge of the pier that ran along the back of the shop.

'You still got the matches?' Mr Seafish asked.

One of the crabs pushed its swollen body half-way into the shop. The door disintegrated around it, sending out a shower of splinters. The creature reached out with its cruel pinchers, trying to burst through the rear window. Adam felt desperately in his right pocket. He had instinctively jammed the matchbox in there when the crab had grabbed him. Fortunately the matches were still in place. Barely hanging on to the railing, he pulled one out.

'I've got them,' Adam said.

The other crab – the one he had shot in the eyes – climbed on top of the first crab and tried to squirm into the shop as well. The shop roof cracked and pitched towards the ocean. Unknown to the crabs, they were both flopping around on top of several litres of kerosene. Adam glanced over at Mr Seafish as he held up the match.

'I am going to strike the match on the count of three,' Adam said. 'Remember to edge towards the front of the pier as soon as the fire starts.'

'I just hope it doesn't explode,' Mr Seafish said.

Adam nodded. 'Then we'll be swimming with the fishes. Get ready. One . . . Two . . . Three!'

Adam struck the match and threw it into the shop.

The kerosene ignited instantly. The flames flew.

In seconds they engulfed the two giant crabs.

Their screeches then were a thing of absolute horror. Adam thought if he lived to be a hundred he would never forget that sound. It seemed to tear through his whole body, threatening to rupture his ears. The fuel did not explode outright but as the fire licked over the monsters' hideous limbs, they began to thrash about furiously and it seemed that the shop would be pushed into the sea. Mr Seafish stared in amazement at the spectacle. Adam had to give him a hard shove in the ribs.

'Get moving!' Adam yelled. 'The whole shop is going to fall in the water.'

Mr Seafish began to pull himself along the railing. Adam was practically on his back he was pushing him so fast. Only two feet from their faces the rear wall of the shop caught fire. Flames danced close to their noses, singing their eyebrows.

'We're not going to make it!' Mr Seafish cried.

'We will make it!' Adam yelled back.

As they passed a window, the glass shattered and a burning claw poked through. Adam had to duck to stop himself from having his head knocked off. For a second he lost his grip on the railing and slipped. Dangling by one hand, his legs thrashed above the ocean far below. The railing pole was moist with the damp evening air. Slowly Adam could feel himself losing his grip. And it seemed to him right then that the ocean below was full of hungry crabs, although he could not actually see any.

He just didn't want to fall in.

Yet it seemed he would.

His right hand slipped to the critical point.

Right then he felt a firm grip fasten on his wrist.

Adam looked up to see Mr Seafish reaching down to him.

'Hold on, son,' he said. 'I'll pull you up as soon as you stop kicking.'

It sounded like an excellent offer. Adam stopped fighting. Mr Seafish was stronger than he would have thought. With one arm, the old guy pulled him all the way back up to where Adam could plant his feet on the pier.

'Thanks,' Adam gasped.

Mr Seafish patted him on the back. 'I still owe you one, Adam.'

But they were far from safe. Now the entire back wall of the shop was engulfed in flames. To edge towards the front of the pier, they had to hang on to the railing but lean way back over the water. That made their hold on the railing precarious – the crabs were still kicking in agony. If a claw should strike their way again, it would be over for them.

Yet, somehow, they made it to the end of the shop.

There they were able to climb back on to the pier.

They had escaped, for the moment.

Four

The fish and chip shop was now a mass of flames. Miss Crank's gift shop had also caught fire. The heat radiating from the inferno was intense – they could not approach within five metres of it. Slowly the crabs were beginning to stop thrashing. Adam felt no sympathy for them, and the absence of sympathy was rare for him. The creatures had surely intended to kill them both.

Yet if Adam did not feel sympathy, he still felt shaken. He had seldom been so close to death, even with all the adventures he had been on since moving to Spooksville the previous summer. Beside him, Mr Seafish shook his head.

'I'm glad I decided to insure my shop last year,' he said. 'I would be in ruins now if I hadn't.'

Adam glanced towards the pier entrance. A third giant crab had lumbered off the beach and on to the sidewalk. It was moving their way, and it looked like it might cut them off like the others had done. Unfortunately Adam had lost his bike in the fire. He had ditched it too close to the shop when they had retreated. Poking Mr Seafish in the side, Adam pointed at the new crab.

'We can't celebrate yet,' he said. 'We still need to make a run for it. Come on!'

Once again they pitted their legs against the approaching monster. But Mr Seafish was still winded from their first attack. Adam could have run faster, but he had to lag behind with Mr Seafish. The poor guy gasped loudly. It was simply against Adam's nature to leave the old man.

Like before, they were not fast enough. The crab climbed on to the pier entrance before they could get clear. Clearly the screams of the other two crabs had not scared this one off. Reaching out with its claws, it moved towards them.

'Oh no,' Adam moaned as they halted.

'What are we going to do now?' Mr Seafish asked. 'We're out of shops and kerosene.'

Adam looked around desperately. His eyes caught on the small motorboat Mr Seafish kept anchored below his shop. It bobbed in the grey water as Adam pointed at it.

'How do you get down to your boat?' Adam asked.

'I use a rope ladder.'

'Where is it?'

'Back in my shop.'

Wonderful – the rope ladder was in ashes. Adam began to panic and had to force himself to remain calm. There was literally nothing else on the pier they could use to slow the giant crab. Yet beyond the monster, he could see Tira and Cindy trying to edge towards them. Adam waved them back and yelled as loudly as he could.

'You can't do anything!' he shouted.

The girls were still on their bikes. Even at this distance, Adam could see their anxiety. They stopped perhaps fifty metres behind the giant crab. If it was aware of them, it showed no sign.

'You have to get off the pier!' Cindy yelled.

'We know that!' Mr Seafish yelled back.

'Go for the boat!' Tira shouted.

'We will!' Adam shouted back.

Mr Seafish looked at him as if he were crazy.

'If you think I am going to jump off the pier, you don't know me,' the old man said to Adam.

'We have no choice,' Adam said as he turned the other way. 'If we can get to the boat, and get the motor started, we can come in anywhere on the shore.'

Mr Seafish chased after him. 'But the water could be full of these monsters!'

'It probably is,' Adam said as they jogged to where the shops were still burning. Strangely, there was no unusual smell from the simmering crabs. Adam would have expected the whole air to be choked with the odour of cooked meat. Adam added, 'But if we can get into the boat quick enough, they won't be able to get us.'

Mr Seafish approached the railing on the far side of the burning shops and looked down at the cold water. The fifteen metres to the surface looked more like fifty. Mr Seafish shook his head as he mentally measured the distance.

'I think the jump could kill me,' he said.

'Nonsense,' Adam said as he climbed on to the railing. 'My friends and I jumped out of the lighthouse when it was on fire. That jump was at least twice this distance.'

'Are you the ones who burned down the lighthouse?'

'Yeah, but we had to. We were fighting a ghost.'

Mr Seafish sighed and looked towards the advancing crab.

'After today I'll believe in ghosts,' he said. 'All right, Adam, I will jump with you. But I have to warn you that sometimes the outboard motor on my boat takes a minute to start. If this crab decides to follow us over the edge, I don't know if we will make it.'

The crab was less than thirty metres away.

It looked exactly like the others.

Odd, thought Adam. He stood atop the railing.

'The sooner we jump the more time we'll have,' he said. 'Let's do it now!'

41

Mr Seafish climbed on to the railing. Adam had to take hold of his arm to give him balance. Mr Seafish glanced over when they were in position. Incredibly, a smile broke over his wrinkled face.

'I used to jump off this pier in the summer all the time when I was your age,' Mr Seafish admitted. 'Used to get into trouble every time. But I never thought I would be doing it in my seventies.'

Adam had to smile, despite the danger.

'Just pretend you're my age right now and you'll be fine,' he said.

Behind them the giant crab raised its pinchers.

Together they jumped over the side.

Adam barely had a chance to register the sensation of falling. But when he hit the water, he certainly felt the cold. It was instantaneous and smothering. Overhead, a couple of metres up, he saw the dull light of the ocean surface. For the moment he forgot about Mr Seafish. He struggled upwards, feeling the weight of his soaked clothes. All he wanted to do was get to the surface and get out of this water!

Adam broke free to the air seconds later.

He waited several anxious seconds for Mr Seafish. The old man came up behind him and surprised him by touching his shoulder. Adam let out a yelp – he thought it was a crab grabbing him.

'Don't do that!' he snapped at Mr Seafish. But he was apologetic when he saw the old man's face fall, 'I thought you were a giant crab.'

Mr Seafish scratched his aged face. 'I didn't know I looked that bad.' He nodded in the direction of the boat, which bobbed up and down less than five metres away. 'We'd better get out of here before our friend decides to join us.'

Adam glanced up and found the giant crab pressed against the railing. Incredibly, it was trying to climb over the barrier. Yet now its bulk worked against it, and its claws were no good for climbing anyway. Each time it tried to get over the railing it slipped back down. But Adam thought it was only a matter of time before it succeeded.

'I think it has already decided to join us,' Adam muttered.

They swam over to the boat. It was fortunate it was close – Adam's hands were already going numb. Yet it was easier for him to climb into the boat than it was for Mr Seafish. But once he was safely aboard, he helped his old friend. Mr Seafish immediately started to fiddle with the outboard motor at the rear of the small craft.

'I'm glad I refuelled this two days ago,' he muttered as he worked.

'So am I,' Adam said as he scanned the beach. The two remaining crabs were still on the sand, apparently undecided as to what to do next. But they had moved close to the pier. As a result the area around the jetty appeared safe. Adam thought if they put ashore beside the jetty they should be able to run into the town and away from the crabs.

Adam noticed a small crowd of people had gathered in front of the shops along Ocean Avenue. They gaped and pointed at them as Mr Seafish fought with the engine. For once, Adam thought, other people would believe the weird adventures they went through in this town.

'The ignition is wet,' Mr Seafish said.

'Do the best you can,' said Adam, straining to sound calm. Overhead the giant crab had managed to get half its body up on the railing. The metal bars were beginning to bend under its great weight. Adam thought of Watch's question.

Where had they come from?

There had to be reasons why they were so big and why they were attacking at this time.

The boat motor roared to life.

Overhead the giant crab balanced on the sagging railing.

'Take us out of here!' Adam shouted.

'Right away, Captain!' Mr Seafish shouted as he swung the outboard motor to the side, pointing them away from the pier. He had already undone the rope that anchored them in place.

They moved none too soon. The moment they escaped the shadow of the pier the giant crab toppled into the water. The splash from its impact actually soaked them - again. Adam watched in horror as it resurfaced and began to thrash in their direction.

'Give it as much gas as possible!' Adam shouted at Mr Seafish. The old guy pulled the throttle back and the tiny motor roared in protest. Yet the front of the boat crested the ocean swells and they raced

45

forwards. The crab began to fall back. For the first time since the second attack of the giant crabs had begun, Adam felt like they would make it.

Then disaster struck and it seemed so unfair. They had tried so hard to get away, neither of them could really believe it when an unlooked-for crab suddenly reared its head above the water just as they neared the jetty. Really, they were five seconds from safety when the monster appeared.

It caught them both completely off-guard. The coloured dome emerged out of nowhere. The moist eyes stared at them with vengeance. They had killed two of its buddies, it seemed to say.

Now it was payback time.

Mr Seafish barely had time to twist the outboard motor to the side. Yet they were running too fast over the water. The abrupt change of direction caused the boat to slip over. One second Adam was sitting in the bow and dreaming of firm shore, and the next he was flying through the air past a pair of clicking claws. Had the boat's angle been slightly different, he would have flown directly into the crab's wide-open mouth.

Again Adam felt the impact of the cold water.

Again he struggled towards the surface.

But he was not alone with Mr Seafish when he reached the fresh air, not this time. The giant crab splashed in the water beside him. Adam tried to turn, tried to swim towards shore. It was only thirty metres away, a distance he could have run in seconds. He looked for Mr Seafish but could not find him. Adam could only hope he had survived the slipped boat.

Then something hard and sharp fastened on Adam's left leg. He felt a painful yank and the water went back over his head. The cold water went into his mouth, into his lungs, and he began to choke. The agony in his chest was unbearable and he feared his heart would explode. More than anything in the whole world he needed to breathe. And still the monster pulled him down.

Down into black depths where humans could not survive.

Down into a place humans had not even imagined.

Adam's last thoughts were of cold and pain.

Then another claw tightened around his neck and all was dark.

Five

When Adam went under with Mr Seafish, Sally, Watch, and Bryce were back down at the beach. They saw it all, and they probably all would have burst into tears if they had been given a chance. But they had returned with Mr Patton and a number of weapons, and they still had two giant crabs to deal with. Mr Patton was carrying an M16 machine-gun, Bryce a flame-thrower. Sally had a grenade-launcher and Watch had brought a high-powered hunting rifle with a laser sighting.

'We are going to make these guys pay,' Mr Patton swore as the giant crab grabbed Adam and Mr Seafish and pulled them under. Mr Patton was wearing his Marine uniform, and his usual closely cropped blonde brillo pad on his head. There was nothing Mr Patton loved more than a battle. His eyes shone as he stared at the two giant crabs that were approaching swiftly from the direction of the pier. Mr Patton was a good guy to have along in such a situation. He was powerfully built and knew how to handle every type of military weapon. He had helped them in the past when they were fighting the Cold People and the No Ones.

'Adam,' Sally gasped in shock.

'Prepare for combat!' Mr Patton snapped at her. 'We will grieve for our fallen comrades later. Sally, load your grenade-launcher. Bryce, light your flame-thrower. Watch, take aim at that first crab. I want to see what damage a high-calibre bullet can do to it.'

His hard words stirred them to action. Each of them prepared for battle. Watch actually dropped to one knee and took aim at the closest crab. It was maybe fifty metres away. With the help of the laser mounted on his telescopic sight, he was able to focus directly on the crab's right eye. Watch had never fired such a high-powered rifle before. He held on tight as he pulled the trigger.

There was a loud bang.

The recoil was strong. It almost knocked Watch over.

Yet the bullet did not put out the giant crab's eye.

Instead they heard a sharp ricochet noise.

The bullet had bounced off the creature's eye.

Watch slowly climbed to his feet and rubbed his bruised shoulder.

'That's weird,' he muttered. 'The bullet should have gone right through its eye.'

Mr Patton nodded grimly. 'We need stronger fire power. Sally, are you ready with the grenade-launcher?'

Sally had also dropped to one knee and was taking aim.

'Weapon is armed and locked on target,' she said.

'Fire!' Mr Patton ordered.

Of course Sally had never fired a grenade-launcher before either. But perhaps because of her fiery temperament, she had a natural feel for dangerous weapons. Her grenade flew straight at the crab's left leg and exploded on impact. The flash of light and the roar of the blast were impressive. The crab's legs shattered; the parts flew off in several directions. The creature as a whole lost all coordination and toppled to its side. As it hit the concrete its huge belly made a sick grinding sound. Yet the beast continued to click with its claws.

'Fire!' Mr Patton ordered Sally again.

Sally hit it with another grenade, and this one exploded directly in its face. The creature lost both its eyes. Finally it went still, yet the last of the giant crabs was closing in on them swiftly. Sally searched frantically in her bag for more grenades and then turned to Mr Patton with worried eyes.

'I seem to be out of ammunition,' she said.

He nodded grimly. 'I only had two grenades in the store. Bryce, it is up to you now. This last fella looks like he means business.'

But Bryce had already jumped in front of the advancing crab. Whatever his faults might have been, cowardice was not one of them. Bryce actually let the crab come within striking distance before he unleashed his flame-thrower. By then it was too late for the creature to retreat. The wave of flame that spread over it from Bryce's attack was devastating. Like the creatures on the pier, this giant crab immediately burst into flames and began to screech fearfully. For several seconds they watched it thrash about helplessly. Finally, thankfully, it went still.

A heavy smoke floated over the beach.

A heavy grief hung over the gang.

Cindy and Tira arrived from the direction of the pier and together each member of the group tried to console the others. Mr Patton didn't disturb their grief. He knew how much Adam had meant to them. Only Watch stood alone, staring out to sea, staring at the dead crabs. He seemed so intent on some deep thought that no one wished to disturb him. Yet when he finally turned and looked at them, they were surprised to see a look of hope on his face.

'I don't think they're dead,' he said.

Sally blinked as she rubbed her face.

'The crabs would not have spared them,' she said flatly. 'They're not known for their forgiving nature.'

Bryce nodded weakly. 'It might be better if we accept that they're gone.'

Watch was unfazed. 'They're gone, that's for sure. But gone is not the same as dead.' He pointed to the last crab they had destroyed, the one Bryce had fried. 'That creature squirmed as it died. It screeched in agony. We all saw that, heard that. It died like a living creature.'

'Yeah?' Cindy muttered, not following what he was saying. She was holding on to Sally, of all people, for support. Watch gestured for them to come closer to the burnt crab. He pointed to the spot where the eyes had been blown away.

'What do you guys see?' he asked.

Sally shrugged. 'Nothing. Missing eyes.'

'What do you smell?' Watch asked.

'Nothing,' Bryce said, light beginning to dawn on his face. 'Yet we should be smelling something.'

'These crabs should stink to high heaven,' Mr Patton agreed.

'But they do not smell at all,' Watch said. 'Their eyes are blown off and they do not bleed at all.

54

That's because they are not real crabs. They are mechanical creatures.'

His words took a moment to absorb.

'That's ridiculous,' Sally said finally. 'Who would have built them?'

'What is ridiculous is the idea of crabs this size,' Watch said. 'Yet they were programmed to behave like the real thing. They screeched when they were injured. They chased after us like they were hungry. But obviously they felt neither pain nor hunger. Yet the people who built them wanted to make us think they were real.'

'Why?' Cindy asked.

'To scare us,' Watch said. 'To scare us badly.'

Sally shook her head. 'No one could have built these. We don't have the technology.'

Watch stared out to sea. '*We* don't have the technology. But someone out there must have it.'

Cindy gently touched his arm, hope in her eyes.

'You are saying there is hope for Adam because there is someone out there?' she asked.

Watch nodded slowly. 'I think the crab captured

Adam and Mr Seafish. Clearly it had no need to eat them.'

'But where would it have taken them?' Cindy asked.

Watch frowned. 'I have no idea. But there must be an underwater civilisation off Spooksville. It would take a sophisticated society to make creatures like these.'

'If Adam and Mr Seafish were not given air in a matter of minutes they will be dead,' Sally said. 'Even if what you say is true, why should this underwater city go out of their way to save them? Especially when these so-called people sent these creatures after us in the first place?'

'I can be sure of nothing,' Watch said. 'But the fact that the giant crabs have an intelligent society behind them gives me hope that Adam and Mr Seafish are still alive. For now, I prefer to cling to that hope.'

'How do you plan to look for the underwater city?' Bryce asked.

'I have a miniature sub at my shop,' Mr Patton said. 'I have saved it for just such a crisis – an attack

56

from sea. It is small but fast and manoeuvrable. It can fire twin torpedoes and has a docking door rigged to its aft side. It would be my pleasure, Watch, to help you find this underwater city and wipe it from the face of the Earth.'

'Since it is under water, we cannot actually wipe it from the face of the Earth,' Watch pointed out.

'Excellent point,' said Mr Patton. 'We will bury it beneath the waves of Neptune. Should I prepare the sub for launch?'

'Yes,' Watch said. 'I want scuba equipment as well. But we must talk to Bum before we set out in search of the underwater city. We must have some idea where to start looking.'

'And what makes you think Bum knows anything about this city?' Sally demanded.

'Bum knows a little something about everything,' Watch said.

Six

They found Bum at their favourite doughnut shop, sitting outside. He was drinking a small carton of milk and reading a paper from the waste bin. Naturally, he had heard in detail about everything that had happened to them that evening. By this time it was already dark. Bum expressed his sorrow for the loss of Adam and Mr Seafish.

'It was brave of Adam to try to rescue the old fella,' Bum said. 'But if I had been him I would have let the crabs get Mr Seafish. I mean, he was old and his fish and chips were not that good anyway.'

'We love his fish and chips,' Sally said.

'That's because you've never been to England where they know how to make the real thing,' Bum said.

'I don't think Adam was thinking about the quality of Mr Seafish's food when he tried to save him,' Cindy said indignantly.

'If he had he would still be alive,' Bum said.

'We're hoping that they're both still alive,' Watch said. 'The giant crabs that attacked this evening were mechanical creatures.'

Bum was interested. 'Really? I wonder if the Mimbas built them.'

'Who are they?' Tira asked, sitting beside Bum on the doughnut shop step. Bum glanced over his shoulder at the rows of doughnuts that he could not afford.

'I would love to tell you the story,' Bum said. 'I think a doughnut or two would give me the necessary strength. A long chocolate one with whipped cream and a buttermilk one with frosted icing. Another carton of milk would also be nice.'

They chipped in together and bought Bum what

he had asked for, then gathered around him as he recounted the tale of the Mimbas.

'I have told you of the ancient war between Atlantis and Lemuria,' he began. 'That was when both great continents were destroyed, largely because of alien intervention and evil rulers' wicked and foolish desires to be immortal. It was at that time, you remember, that the Cold People were created. It was at the same time that the Mimbas came into being. As the two continents were smashed to pieces from earth- and space-launched weapons, huge tidal waves swept the world. In fact, for centuries almost the entire globe was covered with water. The few that survived had to adapt. One such group was the Mimbas.

'They had a beautiful city off the north-east corner of Lemuria, on an island separated from the main continent by only a small distance. Even though the island was small it was mountainous. They had built their main city on top of the peaks. Perhaps they had foreseen the coming war, I don't know. But as the huge waves swept the world, their city managed to survive – just barely. When everything finally settled down, they were surrounded by a slowly encroaching sea. For years they tried to block the approach of the water, but their efforts were in vain. The polar caps were melting – the world water level was rising. They could build as many dykes and dams as they wished – the sea was going to get them one day and they knew it.

'Yet the Mimbas did not want to leave their fair city. So rather than continuing to try to save it from the sea, they prepared it for the sea. They strengthened the glass and stone wall structures so that they could withstand great pressure. They prepared themselves as well as their buildings. Using genetic engineering, over two generations they slowly developed special gills which they grew below and behind their ears. That way they could breathe just as easily in both air and water. Finally, as the years passed, the ocean covered the Mimbas' city and they went right on living.'

Bum paused to point out to the dark sea.

'And they are out there to this day,' he said. 'I wouldn't be surprised if it was them who sent the giant crabs on to the beach.'

'But why?' Watch asked.

'We must have annoyed them somehow,' Bum said. 'Clearly they want us to leave here. I wouldn't be surprised if a hundred giant crabs invade the city tomorrow.'

'The idea doesn't seem to bother you much,' Cindy said, annoyed.

Bum smiled and had a drink of milk.

'When you live out on the streets, one city is as good as another,' he said. 'Hey, would you guys like to buy me another doughnut? Those other two were wonderful.'

'In a minute,' Watch said. 'From your knowledge of the Mimbas, what could we have done to anger them?'

Bum shrugged. 'What do I know about people who live under the sea? They must be a weird lot. Maybe we have been catching too many of their young with our fish hooks, I don't know.'

'But you do know exactly where their city lies, don't you?' Watch persisted.

Bum gestured vaguely. 'No. It's just out there somewhere.'

Sally stared at him. 'No more doughnuts unless you give us a better idea.'

Bum studied the shoreline. 'If you want to search for Adam and Mr Seafish, I would head up the coast a mile and then take a boat out a half mile. Of course, you don't want to dive in the dark.'

'We have a submarine,' Bryce said.

Bum chuckled. 'Why am I not surprised? Can I have that extra doughnut now?'

'In a moment,' Watch said. 'Do the Mimbas still look like us? Even with their gills?'

Bum was thoughtful. 'They did twenty thousand years ago, but they have lived under the sea away from the sun for so long, I would imagine they must have changed quite a bit since then. For all I know they've grown scales.'

Sally groaned. 'I hope not. They probably smell all fishy and everything. Gross!'

'They sent giant crabs to drive us off,' Watch said as he stood and stared out to sea. 'I think their fishy smell is the last thing we have to worry about.'

Cindy also stood up. 'I just hope Adam and Mr Seafish are still alive.'

Bum sounded an ominous note behind them.

'You should be hoping that they are still human,' he said. 'That the Mimbas have not changed them.'

Seven

When Adam came to, he was lying flat on his back and staring at a glass ceiling that seemed to separate him from the largest aquarium he had ever seen. Inside the aquarium were millions of fish, as well as other sea creatures: dolphins, turtles, seals. There was even a giant octopus – Adam had never seen such a huge example of the creature. Yet all of this was floating in a container that seemed to serve as a ceiling for where he was being kept.

Which was where?

Adam sat up with a start and looked around. Mr Seafish snored peacefully on the floor beside him. The old man appeared fine, although there was a bruise above his right eye. For that matter Adam felt OK, for someone who was supposed to be drowned. Yet as he studied the surrounding room he had to wonder if there was something wrong with his brain. For it was not just the ceiling that stared into the aquarium, but three of the four walls. They were practically enveloped by water.

'Wait a second,' Adam said suddenly to himself. 'That isn't an aquarium. That's the ocean itself!'

The fourth wall, the one that did not look out on the water, was light blue and featureless except for a round door and a small white button in the centre. Adam stood up and tried the door and button.

It appeared to be locked.

'Are we prisoners?' Mr Seafish asked from behind him.

Adam turned. 'We're alive, which is more than I expected. How do you feel?'

Mr Seafish put a hand to his head and groaned.

'I don't know. I'm not used to so much excitement,' he said. 'Where are we?'

'Under the ocean – somewhere. The giant crabs must have dragged us here.'

Mr Seafish looked around in wonder. 'But is it possible we died? Could this be heaven?'

Adam laughed. 'This would only be heaven to the owner of a fish and chip shop. No, I think we are both very much alive. I am just not sure if we are going to stay that way.'

At that moment the circular door swung open and a beautiful young girl with white eyes and a flowing blue gown entered. Her skin was incredibly pale; it looked almost translucent, although her long hair was as black as space. Her large clear eyes were fascinating; they seemed to shine with their own light. Below her ears, on either side, were strange skin markings Adam could not figure out. She did not wear jewellery, and if Adam were to guess, he would have said her clothes were waterproof. The gown gave off a faint metallic shine. She did not smile as she stared at them. Indeed, her expression was vaguely angry.

She could not have been older than Adam.

'My name is Claree,' she said in a soft voice. 'I have been sent to welcome you to Mimba, and to see that you are both physically all right.'

'You speak English,' Adam said with surprise.

'Of course. I have watched your television programmes.'

'You have cable down here?' Mr Seafish asked as he stood up.

Claree did not look amused. 'We are familiar with all aspects of your culture. But I have not come to answer all your questions. If you are feeling all right and not in immediate need of food, I will leave you.'

'I'm a little hungry,' Mr Seafish said. 'What do you have to eat?'

'Fish.'

'Just fish?' Mr Seafish asked.

'Raw fish,' Claree said. 'That is all there is to eat in Mimba, unless you would like some seaweed.'

'What we would really like is to be returned to the surface,' Adam said. 'When can we go back home?'

Claree shook her head. 'You will not be going home. No human who comes to Mimba is ever allowed to leave. From now on this will be your world.'

70

'But we can't stay here,' Adam said. 'It is unnatural for us to live underwater.'

'At present it is unnatural for you. But soon you will be changed.'

Adam didn't like the sound of that.

'How will we be changed?' he asked.

In response Claree gave them a closer look at the weird skin markings below her ears. Adam saw that they were not marks at all, but openings of some kind. They looked like gills.

'No thank you,' Adam said quickly. 'We don't need any of those.'

'You will need them to survive here,' Claree said. 'Less than half of our city is air pressured. The rest is underwater. You must learn to breathe underwater if you are to survive.'

'But it would be a lot simpler if you would just let us go,' Mr Seafish said.

'I have told you,' Claree said with a note of impatience. 'No human who comes to Mimba ever returns to the surface. It is too dangerous for us to reveal where our city lies.'

'But you revealed your city just fine when you

71

sent the giant crabs into Spooksville,' Adam said. 'People will know they came from somewhere.'

'We sent the crabs into your city to drive you from it,' Claree said. 'Our first attack has failed but we are preparing a much larger one. Besides, your people are fools. They will think the crabs have a natural origin. They will not realise they have been sent from an underwater city.'

'I figured it out quickly enough,' Adam said.

'Those crabs were not real?' Mr Seafish asked.

'Just machines,' Adam said.

'You only figured that out because you are here,' Claree said. 'Otherwise you would not have guessed.'

'We left friends behind in Spooksville who are pretty smart,' Adam said. 'I wouldn't count on keeping your city a secret much longer.'

Claree turned to leave. 'Soon your city will be empty. That is all that matters.'

Adam stopped her. 'Wait! Why are you doing this to us?'

Claree stared at him with her strange white eyes. 'We rescued you,' she said. 'You should be grateful.'

72

'You attacked us,' Adam said. 'We are not grateful for that. Why do you feel you have to empty our city?'

'Because you attacked us first.'

Adam paused. 'I don't understand. What did we do to you? We didn't even know you were here.'

Claree scowled. 'In your people's arrogance of all things living in the sea you attack us. For twenty thousand years we have lived peacefully off your coast. We have asked nothing from you and have let you carry on as you saw fit. But now you dump tonnes of poisonous chemicals in our sea. Year after year the pollution gets worse. Your own city is one of the worst culprits, especially because it is so close to us. You treat the sea like an open sewer. Finally, though, we have had enough. We are fighting back, and we will not stop the fight until we have driven your people from your city. Then perhaps our water can heal and return to normal.' She turned away again. 'Tomorrow a thousand giant crabs will attack your town. They will not be programmed to spare lives, as they were today. Your city will not survive.'

Adam tried to stop her a second time.

'Wait!' he cried. 'This is insanity. Why didn't you

try to talk to us about the problem first? Before launching an attack?'

Claree was bitterly amused.

'You humans love to talk,' she said. 'You have talked endlessly about the pollution you have dumped in the ocean. Yet you have done little to stop it. Well we do not have an endless amount of time. Our people need the sea to survive. If we sit and wait for your people to make changes, we will be extinct.' She nodded to the door. 'Stand aside. I am leaving and you will not be permitted to leave this room until you have been changed.'

'But we need to discuss this situation,' Adam pleaded. 'I am sure we can come to a reasonable solution. A war between your people and mine can't help anything.'

'It is the only solution. It has already been decided. And then, if the pollution still continues, we may send the crabs into all coastal towns. Your people do not deserve the sea. You do not know how to honour it.'

Claree forced him to move aside and then left the room.

Mr Seafish stared at Adam and then shook his head.

'That is one angry mermaid,' he said.

Adam sighed. 'She sounded more like a shark to me.'

Eight

Mr Patton generously turned the submarine over to them once Watch decided that four of the usual gang should go after Adam and Mr Seafish. Because they had experience in dealing with weird aliens and monsters, Watch wanted to bring Bryce, Sally and Cindy with him. He told Tira and George to stand guard and alert the city if there was another giant crab attack.

Watch also warned Mr Patton that the next attack – if there was one – would probably be much worse. Mr Patton took the warning seriously. He had returned to his weapons catalogues and was trying to order as much heavy artillery as possible.

At present Watch and his pals were cruising in the tiny submarine twenty metres beneath the surface of the ocean. They were close to the spot Bum had pointed out, about a mile north of town, a half mile offshore. The water was dark, naturally, but they had a powerful headlight on the sub and their internal controls were sophisticated. They had high-tech sonar, sensitive acoustical beacons. They could sweep in each direction for attacking crabs. Plus their torpedo tubes were loaded. They could fire off a dozen rounds if they had to.

'Any sign of movement?' Watch asked Bryce. Watch was driving the sub, Bryce was manning the sonar board. Sally was reading a magazine and Cindy was having a nervous breakdown. Cindy didn't like having so much water directly over-head. There were dark windows on all sides of the sub.

'No sign,' Bryce said.

'What is the range of this sub?' Sally asked.

'Over a hundred miles,' Watch said. 'I am increasing our speed. We are moving into deep water. Down to twenty metres.'

'If Adam is down this deep he is dead,' Sally said.

'You're a cheery character,' Cindy snapped.

Sally sighed. 'I am merely suggesting that we don't go searching where there is no possibility of finding our friend.'

'We don't know how the Mimbic technology evolved to counter the pressure of the sea,' Watch said. 'We have to search the whole area.'

'I am picking up something,' Bryce said suddenly.

'What is it?' Sally demanded.

'A metal object, ten metres across,' Bryce said. 'Irregular shape. It could be a giant crab.' He paused. 'It's turning in our direction.'

'Distance?' Watch snapped.

'It's a hundred metres off to our right but closing in on us fast,' Bryce said.

'Arm the torpedoes!' Sally shouted.

'Wait!' Watch said. 'If we fire this close to their city, they might know we are coming. I was hoping to surprise them. Can we out-run this crab?'

Bryce shook his head. 'No way. They move even faster underwater than on land.'

Watch considered. 'Arm two torpedoes.'

Bryce punched a series of buttons. 'Armed and ready to fire.'

'Distance to the target?' Watch asked.

Bryce read off the numbers. 'Fifty metres . . . Forty. It is coming at us fast!'

'Why don't we fire?' Sally demanded.

'Because I want to make sure it is a crab,' Watch said. 'What if it is another sub with people in it?'

'I hardly think that's the case,' Sally grumbled.

'It doesn't matter,' Watch said. 'We cannot shoot at everything that moves down here. We will wait until it is visible.'

'That should be any second now,' Bryce warned.

A huge crab swam into view.

Watch went to shout "fire". He was too late.

The crab smashed the sub with its claws out.

The sub lights failed. A siren sounded in blackness.

Cold water began to squirt into the sub.

There were screams. Maybe they all screamed.

A dull red light went on. Emergency power.

'Evasive!' Watch shouted.

'You're the one who's steering!' Bryce shouted back.

Watch was indeed steering, although it was questionable how well the sub was responding now that it was taking on water. Vaguely, outside the thick glass, they could see the giant crab spinning around for another attack. It seemed as if Watch was straining to aim the front of the sub towards the creature, probably so that they could fire their torpedoes.

'Well we sure know what it is now!' Sally shouted.

'I'm getting cold!' Cindy cried.

'I think it's the water drenching us,' Sally yelled.

'Ready torpedoes,' Watch snapped.

'They are ready,' Bryce said. 'But you have to get our nose up.'

'It wants to go down,' Watch said, fighting with the controls.

'It's the weight of the water,' Bryce said.

'I've already said that,' Sally said.

The crab reached for them once more.

'I am going to give us a jolt of power,' Watch said. 'Fire as I do so.'

'We might miss it,' Bryce said. 'The locking controls are off-line.'

'We destroy it now or it destroys us,' Watch said, fighting his grip on the steering wheel. 'Fire on three. One . . . Two . . . Three!'

Bryce fired the torpedo.

The crab was so close.

It seemed to take the projectile in the face.

There was a flash of light. The shock of an explosion.

The crab seemed to disintegrate before their eyes.

Once again the power failed and they were thrown into blackness. Incredibly the shock wave did not damage the submarine hull further. Yet the icy cold water continued to pour in at a frightening rate. In the dark, with nowhere to run, the sea water could not have been more terrifying.

Finally the dull red emergency lights came back on.

'What is our depth?' Bryce asked.

'We're below forty metres,' Watch said. 'And sinking.'

'You have to blow our tanks,' Bryce said. 'Drive us to the surface.'

'I know,' Watch said quietly.

'We can make the surface?' Cindy asked.

'Yes,' Bryce said a note of desperation entering his voice. 'If we act now and blow our buoyancy tanks. But we have to do so in the next few seconds.' He paused. 'Watch?'

'Yes,' Watch said.

Sally pressed close to Watch. 'Blow our tanks, man! We're sinking!'

'I know,' Watch said.

'Why don't you do it?' Sally screamed at him.

'I am thinking,' Watch said.

'This is no time to think!' Sally yelled. 'We have to get up!'

'I know,' Watch said.

'What are you thinking about?' Cindy asked.

'Adam,' Watch whispered, then he sighed. 'If we blow our tanks we will reach the surface. There we can probably be rescued. But we will not be able to use the sub to get back down here.' He paused. 'We will not be able to rescue Adam and Mr Seafish. It will be over.'

Sally drew in a ragged breath. 'We have no choice. Bryce?'

'I don't think we have any choice,' Bryce said quietly. 'We're taking in too much water too quickly.'

Watch looked at Cindy. 'Cindy?' he asked.

She was shivering badly. 'I don't want to just leave them. But I don't want to die down here.'

Watch gave her a sad smile. 'And down here might be nowhere, I know. It's just that I thought if the crab was nearby, maybe the Mimbas were as well.' Watch reached for the button that would blow the tanks. 'But I guess that was just wishful thinking.'

The submarine suddenly bumped into something.

They all peered out of the dark windows.

They were surprised to see light.

They were even more surprised to see Adam and Mr Seafish.

Nine

Adam and Mr Seafish were even more surprised to see the gang. Especially trapped in a small submarine that was obviously flooding. Of course the sub was lying somewhere up on the ceiling. Adam and Mr Seafish could not exactly climb up and have a conversation with them.

'They look like they're sinking,' Adam said, his head tilted back.

'They look like they've already sunk,' Mr Seafish said. 'I don't suppose they brought any food with them?'

'If they did it's wet by now,' Adam said. 'They're going to have to get out of that sub.' Adam waved and gestured to his friends. Then he made a choking gesture and pointed to them again. Naturally his friends appreciated him pointing out the fact that they were about to drown. But what Adam was actually trying to do – with his next gesture – was convince them to move to the side of his oversized cage, where he hoped there was an entrance of some kind. Adam just wanted the sub off the ceiling. He was sure it would only make Claree's bad mood worse.

Watch seemed to have power left in the sub. Twisting the steering wheel to the side, the sub began to crawl over the ceiling. Finally it moved out of view, but not before Adam saw a sight he never thought he would in his life. Cindy and Sally were hugging in joy.

Adam guessed they were glad to see him alive.

'I hope they're able to rescue us,' Adam said.

'They're the ones who look like they need rescuing,' Mr Seafish said.

Adam nodded reluctantly. 'I suppose we have to take care of ourselves. But I just can't figure out a way to get through that door.'

'That Claree knows how to get in and out of here,' Mr Seafish said. 'I say we jump her and force her to let us out next time she shows her face here.'

'That might create a bad impression.'

Mr Seafish was unmoved. 'Why do we have to worry about what kind of impression we create? She is the one who is keeping us captive! It is also her kind that plans to destroy our city.'

'Yeah. But according to her, we have been destroying her city all along.'

'With a little pollution? That's nonsense!'

Adam shook his head. 'No. I think she was telling us the truth there. But I agree we might have to force her to our will. But let me do it, I don't want her getting hurt.'

'But remember, Adam you are going to have to scare her,' Mr Seafish warned. 'You can't be too timid.'

'I know,' Adam said. He was not looking forward to it.

Claree returned twenty minutes later with a bowl of soggy fish for Mr Seafish. She had not brought one for Adam, perhaps because he had not said he was hungry. Or maybe because she just didn't like him. She liked him a lot less when he cornered her as she tried to leave.

'You can't just walk out of here,' he said as he blocked her way.

She was annoyed. 'You are in no position to give me orders.'

'But we are in an excellent position,' Adam said in a serious voice. 'There are two of us and only one of you.'

She allowed an arrogant chuckle. 'You are a fool! I have studied your species. You are merely bluffing.'

Mr Seafish put down his bowl of food and stepped behind her.

'Captive humans do not bluff,' he said darkly.

'We do not wish to hurt you,' Adam said. 'We would rather work out our troubles around a bargaining table. But since you insist that war is the only solution, then we must prepare ourselves to do whatever is necessary to escape.'

Claree seemed unsure of herself. 'You will never escape from here,' she said quietly.

Adam took a step towards her. 'Then we will die trying. And you will die if you try to stop us.'

Claree swallowed. 'You would not harm me. Even you are not that barbaric.'

Adam came very close to her, kept his eyes drilled on hers.

'You should have watched more of our shows,' he said. 'Humans have no trouble behaving like animals when they have been cornered. You have cornered us. Now I want you to open that door for us. If you do not, you will not leave this room. Do you understand?'

She tried to force a smile, but failed miserably.

'I say,' she repeated, 'that you are bluffing.'

Mr Seafish grabbed her from behind, by the neck.

Adam felt sick to his stomach but shook his head dangerously.

'He will break your neck if that door is not open in five seconds,' Adam said.

Claree had a change of heart.

She opened the door for them.

And Adam and Mr Seafish saw Mimba.

Ten

Watch and his fellow submarine mates found an opening into Mimba not far from the glass cage where Adam and Mr Seafish were being kept. Actually, it was better than a mere opening – it was practically a safe harbour for the submarine. At least for a little while. As they floated up into the strange room, fortunately there was no one around.

Yet as they climbed out of the sub, Watch could see the chamber was not designed merely to receive boats. The Mimbic culture was a cross between water and air. Where the air ran out there was no barrier. The Mimbas just dived in and kept moving. The planks in the chamber were sidewalks, but they did not end when the planks did. Watch suspected the whole city moved effortlessly from water back to air and then back again to water.

'I want to take a gun with us,' Sally said as they climbed out of the sub. She reached for Mr Patton's personal M16 but Watch stopped her.

'There will be no shooting down here,' he said.

'For your information you have already fired off a torpedo,' Sally said.

'That was in self-defence against an attacking creature,' Watch said.

'That creature came from this place,' Sally said. 'It was programmed to kill us by the people who live down here.'

Watch would not let her take the gun.

'We are not going to let your famous trigger finger start the next world war,' Watch said. 'The gun stays here.'

'But this sub is going to sink in a few minutes,' Sally complained.

'No it won't,' Bryce said as he secured the sub

with some rope. 'I have turned the damaged side up. We should still be able to ride it to the surface.'

'Good,' Cindy said. 'Let's get Adam and Mr Seafish and let's get out of here.'

'We need to rescue our friend,' Watch agreed. 'But we also need to find out why the Mimbas are attacking.'

'Why don't we also try to find the cure for the common cold while we're here,' Sally said. 'We're doing everything else.'

'Maybe they do know how to cure colds,' Watch said.

They exited the watery room into a huge dome of soft blue light. The dimensions of this structure were hard to guess; it was as if the dome were miles across. In the distance they could see monorail-like devices. There even seemed to be a park of some kind. Certainly, within the one huge dome were many small ones and thousands of Mimbas. Yet the first people the gang bumped into were Adam and Mr Seafish. They had a young girl with them. Cindy and Sally both pushed her out of the way as they leapt to hug Adam.

'We thought you were dead!' Cindy cried.

'We were already planning your funeral!' Sally agreed.

Adam laughed. 'Such reports were completely premature. What, you thought one giant crab could get me down?'

'It got you,' Claree said darkly. 'You're here, aren't you?'

Sally sniffed. 'And who is this charming young fish?'

Adam nodded. 'Guys, meet Claree. She is a Mimba, obviously, and has been put in charge of us.'

'Why did they put a kid in charge of you two?' Cindy wondered aloud.

'Because we know from studying your culture that the very young and the very old of your society are not capable of seriously dangerous acts,' Claree explained.

Sally laughed. 'You haven't studied us much, my dear. We are not normal kids anyway. We are from Spooksville and we don't like to be pushed around. So you be careful around us.'

'We're the ones who have to be careful,' Adam said. He went on to explain about the impending attack. The others listened with grim faces. When Adam was done he turned to Claree. 'You have to help us stop this attack. It will only end in disaster.'

Claree snorted. 'I have waited for this attack all my life. I think it is years overdue. Why should I help you destroy my world?'

'But what if we promise to help protect your world once we return to the surface?' Adam asked.

'That's just more human talk,' Claree said. 'It means nothing to me.'

'When did this last wave of pollution start?' Watch asked her.

'When your people developed a technological society,' Claree said. 'And I know you will not give up that society to save us.'

'No,' Watch said. 'That is not what I meant. From what you and Adam have said, you have implied there was a huge upsurge in pollutants just recently. I am sure that is what has inspired your people to take such drastic action. When did it start?'

Claree thought for a moment.

'I know the Council convened a special meeting to address the problem this time last year,' she said. 'For some reason, right then, the water around here turned particularly bad.'

Watch considered. 'The paint factory off Rocky Cliff opened just over a year ago. I have heard rumours that they have been dumping chemicals in the sea. I even heard that the Mayor in town tried to close them down but then they bought them off. The company is called Glow Bright.'

'But don't paints have lead in them and stuff like that?' Cindy asked.

'Yes,' Watch said. 'None of their waste should go into the sea but that must be what's happening. Claree, what if we make a deal with you and your people? We will help get Glow Bright closed down if you will postpone your attack?'

Claree shook her head. 'My people will never agree to that. You can try to close the factory but somebody with money will just come along and buy off another one of your politicians. The factory will reopen. All humans can be bought.'

'We cannot be bought,' Cindy said.

'Not unless the price is really exceptional,' Sally said.

'The factory cannot reopen if it does not exist,' Watch said. 'What if we agree to destroy it ourselves? Your people should notice an almost immediate drop in pollution. Would that be enough to stop them from attacking our city?'

'Wait a second,' Adam said. 'We're just a bunch of kids. We can't blow up a factory.'

'We must take drastic steps if the very ocean is in peril,' Watch said. 'I would feel perfectly clear in my conscience blowing up that factory – as long as no one was inside at the time. It is a menace to our people and to the Mimbas. What do you say, Claree?'

She was interested. 'Can you put it out of order tonight?'

'Yes,' Watch said.

She hesitated. 'I cannot swear to you that my people will now allow the attack still to go forward. As a race you are all polluters.'

Bryce spoke up. 'As a protector of my race, I cannot leave here with a thousand dangerous giant crabs functioning and ready to attack. Watch, I will not leave here until they have been disabled. It is too risky for humanity. The Mimbas could change their mind about us at any time.'

'But we can make a deal,' Watch said.

'A deal is better than a fight,' Adam said.

'We can make a stronger deal with strength on our side,' Sally said. 'I agree with Bryce. We cannot leave the threat of the giant crabs hanging over us.'

'I agree,' Mr Seafish said. 'I don't want to have to eat raw fish for the rest of my life.'

'You are not going to have to eat raw fish no matter what happens,' Watch said.

'Who knows what will happen if those giant crabs attack humanity?' Mr Seafish asked seriously. 'We might never recover. I say let's waste them while we're down here.'

'I don't know what to do,' Cindy said. 'I just know that I'm cold.'

'I will not help you destroy our army,' Claree

said, throwing Sally an angry look. 'We only built it to protect ourselves.'

'Yeah, it looks really friendly when it pops out of the sea and flexes its claws,' Sally snickered.

'Listen,' Adam said. 'We have to work together, both sides and all us humans. OK, so the crabs are scary. They pose a continuing threat. We're not going to be able to swim around down here and destroy each and every one of them.'

'They must be controlled from a central place,' Watch said reluctantly. 'If we found that control place, and put it out of action, I suspect all the crabs would freeze up.' He glanced at Claree as he spoke but her eyes were staring at the floor.

'This is how you would help us?' she said bitterly.

'We will still destroy the paint factory,' Watch promised.

'When we get around to it,' Sally muttered.

'No,' Adam said firmly. 'The pollution must stop tonight.'

'Then we are agreed,' Bryce said. 'We take the submarine out of here, destroy their control centre, then go after the factory?'

'We do not know where the control centre is,' Adam said.

'It is probably located between the jetty and the pier,' Watch said, 'on the floor of the ocean. Seeing as it was designed to launch an attack on Spooksville. That is also where the first giant crabs appeared. Am I right, Claree?'

Her face fell, but she shook her head tightly.

'I will not tell you,' she said angrily.

Adam spoke carefully. 'You are going to have to come with us, Claree. You will need to verify for your people that we kept our end of the bargain.'

'And we're not going to let you out of our sight anyway,' Sally muttered.

Claree lashed out with her voice. 'What bargain? You have not even discussed it with my people! You have just decided that it is fair!'

'But it is fair,' Bryce said. 'If the pollution stops you don't need your giant crabs. We will stop the pollution and the crabs – it is very simple.'

Claree gave him a dark look then smiled thinly.

'You think you can knock out our army so easily?' she said. 'You will all be in for a surprise. Yes, you will all wish you were Mimbas. You will wish that you knew how to breathe underwater.'

Eleven

The submarine was not going to sink with them in it. That was Bryce's opinion, after he had found some goo in a storage closet belonging to the Mimbas. He had applied it to the crack caused by their latest giant crab attack and the stuff had hardened in seconds.

'Even though it was all wet in here,' he said as they pulled out of Mimba city. 'Amazing.'

'We are used to dealing with the wet,' Claree said bitterly. She was stuck in the back between Cindy and Sally. Adam and Watch did not approve – they thought it was rude to treat their guest that way – but Bryce did not want her anywhere near the controls.

105

'But you must get tired of eating raw fish,' Sally said. 'When you study our TV programmes and see all the food commercials doesn't it make you want to come out of the sea and order a pizza?'

'My people have existed for twenty thousand years with a high degree of civilisation,' Claree said. 'Your civilisation has barely begun and already it has come close to wiping itself out. Your special foods are nothing. Your whole society is like a cancer.'

Sally made a face. 'Pizza's not that bad.'

'But there must be some aspects of our culture you admire?' Cindy asked gently.

Claree looked up sharply at the question. It was as if she was going to snap at Cindy. But then all she did was lower her head and shake it sadly.

They ploughed through the dark water, leaving Mimba city behind. Although they were not at present taking on more water, it was still damp and crowded inside the sub. Plus Watch was running the sub with the headlights off. He wanted to find the control base for the crabs with sonar. He wanted the Mimbas to have no warning that they were going to be attacked.

'We should be passing the pier about now,' Watch said fifteen minutes later. 'Bryce, begin your sonar sweeps of the floor of the sea.'

'Aye Captain,' Bryce said.

'And don't call me that,' Watch muttered.

'I have to call you something.'

'Call me Watch.'

'How about Captain Watch?'

'That would be OK. Have you spotted anything?'

'Not yet. Wait!' Bryce fiddled with the controls. He turned around with excitement. 'It is as we suspected. There is a medium-sized dome fifty metres in front of us. It is on the floor of the ocean at a depth of thirty metres.'

'Arm torpedoes!' Sally shouted.

'Wait,' Adam said. He turned to Claree. 'Are there people aboard that control centre?'

She would not look at him.

'What do you care?' she asked.

'We don't want to kill anyone,' Watch said.

Claree raised her head. 'There are a dozen people aboard the control centre,' she said.

'She is lying,' Bryce said. 'The control centre would almost surely be automated. She just doesn't want us to attack it.'

'But we can't be sure,' Adam said.

'I am sure,' Bryce said. 'The Mimbas are not there. And we have to do this. Maybe they will appreciate that we have closed the paint factory, maybe they won't. But we can't worry about giant crabs grabbing us every time we go for a walk on the beach.'

Adam turned to Watch. 'What do you think?' he asked.

Watch hesitated. 'What Bryce says is logical. But it is hard to be sure. I hate just to open fire on it.'

'But they can live even at these depths,' Sally said. 'Even if we destroy it, they should be able to get out alive.'

Watch nodded. 'With a little warning. I could fire off a warning torpedo.'

'I don't recommend that,' Bryce said as he stared at the small blue screen in front of him.

'Why not?' Adam demanded.

Bryce's voice jumped a notch. 'Because there are

several giant crabs right in front of us! Watch! Hard to port!'

Watch immediately wrenched the sub hard over on its side. Now the battle was on. Obviously the crabs did not need light to lock on to them but light was still a help for human eyes and aim. Watch turned the sub's headlights on and they were stunned by the horror of the sight of dozens of giant crabs swimming frantically towards them, their pinchers stretched out.

'Arm torpedoes!' Watch shouted to Bryce. 'Fire at will!'

'Firing torpedoes!' Bryce shouted back.

The sub shuddered as the weapons launched.

There was an explosion of light and sound.

Giant crabs turned to scrap metal.

The shock waves rocketed them.

'Two giant crabs directly below us!' Bryce shouted.

'Coming around!' Watch yelled as he fought with the steering wheel, which not only moved right and left but up and down as well. 'Arm more torpedoes!'

'Armed and ready!' Bryce yelled.

'Fire!' Watch said.

The torpedoes streaked through the watery black. There were another two explosions of colour and noise. It appeared as if half-a-dozen crabs blew up this time. It seemed that nothing could stop them from reaching their goal. Bryce sent off another barrage of torpedoes, and still another. The ocean literally churned with pieces of the enemy, and still the sub roared toward the control centre.

Then a giant crab came at them from above.

It came so fast and hard it made them all gasp.

'Watch!' Bryce shouted.

'Load another torpedo!' Watch shouted back as he tried to get the nose of the sub in front of it. But the crab already had its claws on their roof and it seemed the shooting was over for now.

'I am out of torpedoes,' Bryce said.

'How are we going to destroy the control centre without torpedoes?' Sally demanded. 'You should have saved one.'

'If I had one right now I would use it on this guy,' Bryce said.

The crab tightened its grip.

They could see its huge mechanical eyes, gloating over them.

Icy water began to squirt into the cabin.

'Not again,' Cindy moaned.

The submarine began to sink.

'What are we going to do?' Adam asked Watch desperately.

'I am thinking,' Watch said.

'Please think quickly and clearly,' Sally suggested.

'We are going down fast,' Bryce said. 'The pressure is building. The sub could explode any second. We have to blow our tanks and hope we can make the surface.'

'We will never make the surface with that crab holding us down,' Adam said. 'Watch?'

'I am still thinking,' Watch said. 'How many scuba sets do we have?'

'Five sets,' Cindy said.

'But there are seven of us,' Bryce said.

'Six humans,' Sally corrected. 'Miss Fish here doesn't need scuba.'

'Shut up, you guys,' Watch said. 'Then get your

hands away from anything metal. I am going to short our batteries through the length of the submarine hull. It should throw off the crab.'

'Can you do that?' Bryce asked.

'Yeah. They did it on an old episode of *Voyage to the Bottom of the Sea*,' Watch said. 'Once the crab is off us, I am going to set the sub on a collision course with the control centre. Just before impact I want you guys to open the sub hood and jump out. I will give you the signal when.'

'But you will be drowned!' Cindy protested.

'I might make it to the surface,' Watch said.

'Not from thirty metres down,' Bryce said.

'We have no choice,' Watch said. 'This is my plan and it is a good one. You guys get suited up now!'

While the others began to wriggle into their scuba gear, Adam moved close to where Watch was continuing to struggle with the steering-wheel. Adam spoke quietly so that the others could not overhear.

'I can hold my breath longer than you,' Adam said.

'Since when?' Watch asked.

'You know it's true. I'm in better shape than you. I should be the one to try to make it to the surface without the scuba equipment.'

'No,' Watch said. 'It's too risky.'

'Like it's better for you to die than me?' Adam asked.

'I'm not going to die.'

'You might. As the sub heads for the control centre, you're a busy man. You have to get the crab off us and you have to keep the sub on target. But I am just sitting here doing nothing. I can be taking deep breaths. I can be preparing to make it to the surface. If it is me, at least there is a chance I will make it. There is no way you will make it. For that reason you have to take the last set of scuba gear.'

Watch stared at him. 'You are just trying to be a hero.'

'I am not trying to be a hero. I already am a hero many times over. You take the scuba gear, you will need it to breathe. It's bad enough that you're going to lose your glasses and not be able to see anything.'

Watch glanced at the others. 'I have always had

a fear of drowning. Don't you have the same fear?'

Adam lied. 'No. It doesn't scare me at all.'

'You're lying.'

'You can tell?'

'Yes. It's obvious. Are you sure you want me to take the gear?'

'Maybe I can share it with you.'

'You cannot share it. It will be every man for himself when we bail out.'

'But what if you lose your direction towards the surface?'

'I will follow my bubbles, don't worry,' Adam said.

Watch smiled and patted his friend on the back.

'You are so brave, you shame me. But you are right – I will be busy up until the last second. But if you drown, you know Sally will blame me for the rest of my life.'

'Then I must live so that she doesn't yell at you all those years.' Adam handed him the scuba gear. 'Good luck, Watch.'

'Good luck to you, Adam.'

The gang got suited up, each with a regulator in

their mouths except for Claree and Adam. They pressed their hands on to their rubber suits while Watch got ready to short the hull.

'There should just be a few sparks,' he said as he momentarily took his regulator out of his mouth. 'But no pain for us if we're not touching any metal.'

'What if we accidentally do touch some metal?' Cindy said.

'Then you will die,' Watch said.

'Break it to us gently,' Sally said.

It was time.

The crab's pinchers were all over them.

Watch shorted the sub's hull.

Sparks flew. The giant crab screeched.

Then it let go of them. They stopped sinking.

Watch shot them forward, in the direction of the crab control centre. The engines revved; he had them set at high power. Yet the sea water now gushed in, weighing down their cabin and their hearts. The others glanced anxiously in Adam's direction but could say nothing with their regulators in their mouths. Adam flashed them a weak thumbs up. Without even a wet suit, he was shivering to death.

Claree kept her head down, lost in thought.

A dome of faint blue light appeared out of nowhere.

Watch pressed a lever. There was a loud hiss of air.

Then the ocean landed in Adam's lap.

The pressure was immediate and intense. His ears almost exploded inside his head. Adam could not believe the sense of confusion he had right then. Everything was pitch black and freezing cold and there wasn't a chance in heaven or hell that he could follow his bubbles to the surface because he could not see a thing. He could hardly feel his hands or feet any more, and he had only been out of the sub for a few seconds.

Actually, he was still in the sub but didn't know it. Not until a pair of gentle but firm hands grabbed him and pulled him out of the racing vehicle. It was lucky they did, for a second later the sub hit the control centre. There was another explosion of light and sound. It was blinding yet it did nothing to help point him towards the surface. The hands on him did, however.

They did even more than that.

The mind behind them. The face.

Adam felt a figure lean over him in the cold darkness and breathe warm air into his lungs. With a shock he realised it was Claree. She was trying to save his life. Him, a miserable human being who had helped pollute her world. He did not understand why she was saving him, he only knew that he needed her to stay close to him if he was going to reach the surface, and the shore beyond.

The surface came slowly but safely.

The shore came just as easily, with her help.

Epilogue

Later that same extraordinary night, when they were floating in a hot air balloon above the Glow Bright paint factory and getting ready to destroy it with a pair of Mr Patton's very special plastic explosive bombs, Adam turned to Claree and asked her why she had bothered to save him. She took a minute before she replied. She had been staring off into the distance, not at the sea but at the stars. The wind had finally blown away the clouds.

'Why were you so surprised?' she asked as she turned towards him.

The others in the gondola were fussing with the explosives. Mr Patton was barking orders and looking excited. They had a moment to themselves.

'Because you blamed us for everything that is wrong in your world,' Adam said. 'Last thing I expected was for you to help me.'

Claree nodded. 'But then I saw how you were willing to risk your life to save your friends. You know that is one of two things that I admire most about you humans. That your life is often at its best when it looks like it's going to end.'

'What is the other thing you admire?' he asked.

She turned and stared at the night sky, and Adam could not help but notice the great longing on her face.

'Your people have the stars,' she said simply.

He did not disturb her again. He just let her enjoy the view. Why, she did not even look down when the factory was wiped out.

If you enjoyed ATTACK OF THE GIANT CRABS
you'll love Christopher Pike's other Spooksville chillers . . .

Spooksville

The Haunted Cave

There's a famous cave outside Spooksville. Adam, Sally, Watch and Cindy can't wait to explore it. But that's a big mistake.

The moment they enter the cave, the entrance closes behind them.

They're trapped in darkness.

Then they realise that something is following them. Something big, black and very hungry . . .

Spooksville
CHRISTOPHER PIKE

❏	72441 2	Alien Invasion	£3.50
❏	72442 0	The Evil House	£3.50
❏	72443 9	Invasion of the No Ones	£3.50
❏	72444 7	Time Terror	£3.50
❏	72445 5	The Thing in The Closet	£3.50
❏	72446 3	Attack of the Giant Crabs	£3.50
❏	72658 X	Night of the Vampire	£3.50
❏	72659 8	Dangerous Quest	£3.50

All Hodder Children's books are available at your local bookshop, or can be ordered direct from the publisher. Just tick the titles you would like and complete the details below. Prices and availability are subject to change without prior notice.

Please enclose a cheque or postal order made payable to *Bookpoint Ltd*, and send to: Hodder Children's Books, 39 Milton Park, Abingdon, OXON OX14 4TD, UK. Email Address: orders@bookpoint.co.uk

If you would prefer to pay by credit card, our call centre team would be delighted to take your order by telephone. Our direct line *01235 400414* (lines open 9.00 am–6.00 pm Monday to Saturday, 24 hour message answering service). Alternatively you can send a fax on *01235 400454*.

TITLE		FIRST NAME		SURNAME	

ADDRESS	
DAYTIME TEL:		POST CODE	

If you would prefer to pay by credit card, please complete:

Please debit my Visa/Access/Diner's Card/American Express (delete as applicable) card no:

Signature ....

Expiry Date: ....

If you would NOT like to receive further information on our products please tick the box. ❏